Library of Congress Cataloging-in-Publication Data Available

10 9 8 7 6 5 4 3 2 1

Published in 2001 by Sterling Publishing Co., Inc.
387 Park Avenue South, New York, NY 10016

Originally published in Great Britain under the title Rory's Story by Brimax,
an imprint of Octopus Publishing Group Ltd
2-4 Heron Quays, London E14 4JP

Distributed in Canada by Sterling Publishing
c/o Canadian Manda Group, One Atlantic Avenue, Suite 105
Toronto, Ontario, M6K 3E7, Canada

Printed in Italy

Sterling ISBN 0-8069-7843-0

Wilbur Waited

Wilbur was not happy.
He had a new *baby sister*,
and she wasn't any fun.
She was small and cried a lot,
and didn't do much except wave her
little, clenched paws in the air.
She was too young to play with him, and
his mother and father were always *busy*.

"Will you cuddle me?" asked Wilbur.
"Soon," said Mother Tiger.
"First I have to feed the baby."
Wilbur waited.
"Will you cuddle me now?" asked Wilbur.
"Soon," said Mother Tiger.
"First I have to wash the baby's ears."
Wilbur waited.

"Will you give me a ride on your back?"
asked Wilbur.
"Soon," said Mother Tiger.
"First I have to give the baby her bath."
Wilbur waited.
"What about now?" asked Wilbur.
"Soon," said Mother Tiger.
"First I have to find the baby's duckie."
"That's my duckie," sighed Wilbur,
as he went to find his father.

"Will you climb a tree with me?"
Wilbur asked Father Tiger.
"Soon," said Father Tiger.
"First I have to finish tidying the den."
Wilbur waited.

"Will you climb a tree now?"
asked Wilbur.
"Soon," said Father Tiger.
"First I have to teach the *baby* how to growl."
"She's so small she can't even growl right,"
sighed Wilbur, as he went to find his friend.

Wilbur met Hippo bouncing along the path.
"Hi!" said Hippo.
"Let's play a game!"
"Okay," said Wilbur, feeling a bit better.
"We could play checkers or chess or...

Crocodiles!"

The rules of Crocodiles are very complicated:

Hippo pretends
to be a crocodile
chasing Wilbur.

Wilbur pretends
to be a crocodile
chasing Hippo.

The two friends run in circles
until they fall over.

Suddenly, Mother Tiger opened the door.
She was angry.
"Shh, you boys!" she said.
"You are making too much noise.
Now the baby is awake and crying."

Mother Tiger went back indoors.
Wilbur felt like crying, too.

"Let's take a look," said Hippo.
"I haven't seen your new baby sister yet."
They tip-toed inside.
Mother Tiger was holding the baby
and singing softly to her.

"Hush little tiger, don't growl and cry,
Mama's going to sing you a lullaby.
The jungle is green, the sky is blue,
Your brother Wilbur wants to cuddle you."

"But I don't know how," said Wilbur.
"It's easy," said Mother Tiger.
"Let me show you."
Mother Tiger put the soft, warm baby
in Wilbur's arms.
Suddenly, Wilbur's baby sister was
all cuddled up on his lap.
The baby smiled.
Wilbur smiled back.

Wilbur's sister made a gurgly growl
and clasped his paw tight.
Then she closed her eyes and fell asleep.

Wilbur and Hippo tip-toed back outside.
"Your sister's nice," said Hippo.
"She can play Crocodiles with us."
"Soon," Wilbur whispered.

Wilbur told all his friends in the jungle
about his new baby sister.
"She's soft and warm!" he said.
"She can clench her fists!" he smiled.
"And she's got a gurgly growl!" he grinned.
"And one day when she's older,
I'll teach her all the things I know."

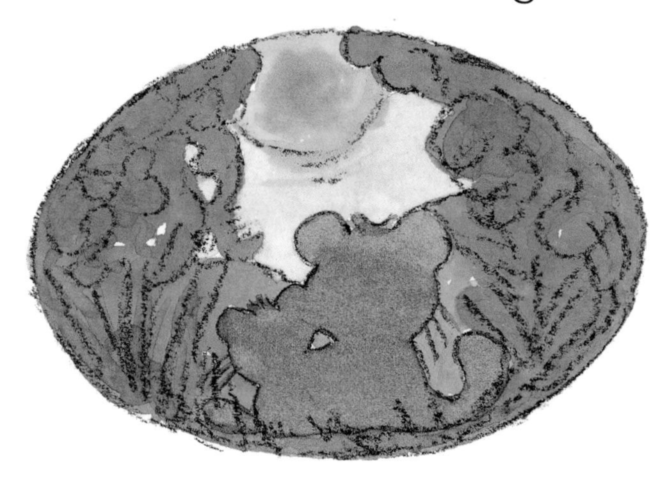

Wilbur dreamed of the great adventures
they would soon have together.
But for now, smiling, Wilbur waited.